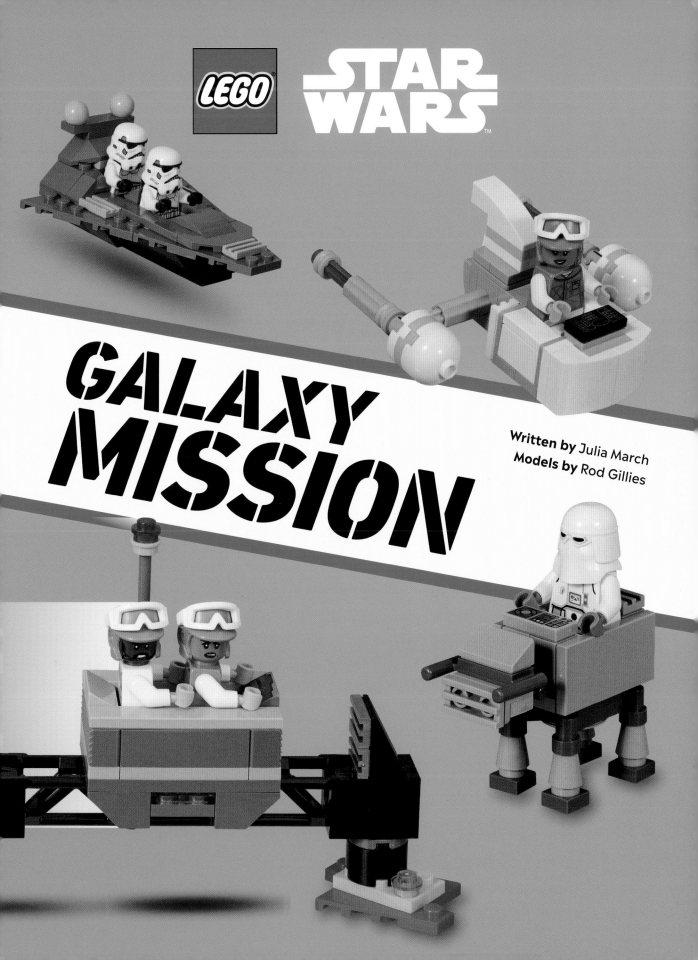

LEGO Star Wars

GALAXY MISSION

Written by Julia March

Models by Rod Gillies

CONTENTS

LET'S JET OFF ON A MISSION!

SPECIAL MISSION

A minifigure is in trouble! Kori Zaran has crash-landed in an asteroid field and needs to get back to her friends at the Hoth Rebel base. Use your LEGO® collection and your building skills to help her navigate around sneaky stormtroopers, dodge dragonsnakes, trick Jawas, cross boiling lava, and much more. Will she make it home safely?

BIG CHALLENGE

It's a long way from the asteroid field to the Rebel base on Hoth. Plus there are a lot of obstacles that stand in her way. It will take skill for this minifigure to build her way home. She can definitely use your help.

BUILDING THE GALAXY AT HOME

See if you can play out this adventure in your own home! Maybe a white sheet could be a snowy Hoth landscape, or your chairs could become asteroids to hop between. There is no limit when it comes to your imagination!

PREPARE FOR YOUR MISSION

Here are some handy tips for building your way through any LEGO mission.

USE YOUR IMAGINATION

If you don't have a particular piece, think about other elements you can use instead.

ORGANIZE YOUR BRICKS

Sort your collection by colors and types before you build. This will save time when you start building.

DON'T WORRY!

If your model doesn't turn out the way you wanted, start again or transform it into something else. The most important part of the mission is to have fun!

MEET KORI ZARAN

Kori has crash-landed on a distant asteroid. Her goal is to get back to the Rebel base on Hoth and complete a high priority galaxy mission on the way. She'll need some special equipment and plenty of help with ideas and building to get there.

Helmet and goggles protect Kori during her mission

I'M READY FOR THIS GALAXY MISSION!

Hoth Rebel clothing is comfortable and warm

MISSION EQUIPMENT

Every adventurer in the galaxy needs the right tools. Kori has some useful gear to help her on her mission home.

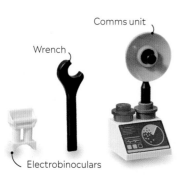

Wrench

Comms unit

Electrobinoculars

Battery pack

Heat pack

MEET THE ADVENTURERS

A mission can be hard work, but it is much easier with friends to help! Meet some of the characters that help Kori along the way. Then spot them in the adventure on the pages that follow.

OREN COLE

Oren is a fellow Rebel on an urgent mission. He and Kori team up to finish the job, get back to the Rebel base on Hoth, and have lots of fun!

R2-Z2C

This friendly astromech has been abandoned in the wreckage of a ship. It uses its technological expertize to advise Kori on useful builds for her journey.

LET'S GO!

HOW TO BUILD!

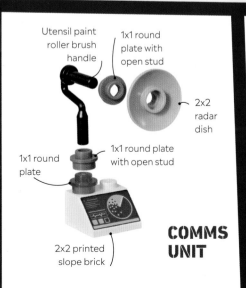

Utensil paint roller brush handle

1x1 round plate with open stud

2x2 radar dish

1x1 round plate

1x1 round plate with open stud

2x2 printed slope brick

COMMS UNIT

BATTERY PACK

1x2/1x2 inverted bracket

1x2 plate with bar

1x2 printed tile

1x2 grille tile

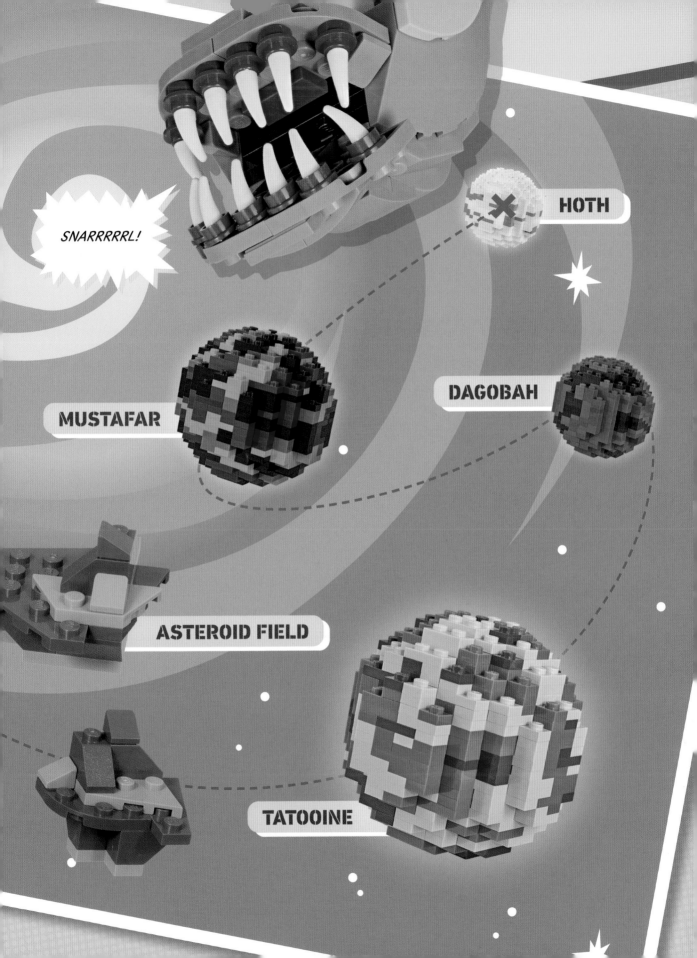

CRASH-LANDING

Rebel Trooper Kori has crash-landed on an asteroid! The only way off it is through a field of whizzing rocks. Kori's ship is in pieces, and she can't call the Rebels for help because her comms unit isn't working. She will just have to build a new vehicle.

THE PLAN = ?

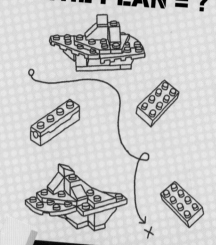

! OBSTACLES

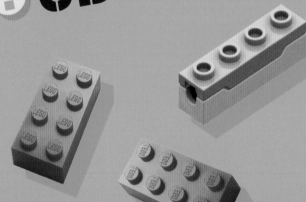

ASTEROIDS

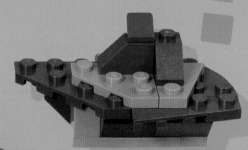

CRASHED SHIP DEBRIS

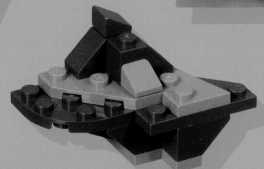

USEFUL BRICKS

1X2/1X2 INVERTED BRACKET

1X1 PLATE WITH RING

1X1 SLOPE

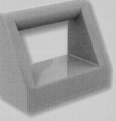

1X2 TILE WITH BAR

BUILDING IDEAS

FAST
LANDSPEEDER

HOW CAN I GET OFF THIS ROCK?

AGILE
HOVERBOARD

...THAT'S IT!

Kori builds a hoverboard that's fast and nimble. She jumps on and weaves her way through the asteroid field. Easy-peasy! But wait, what's that up ahead? One of the asteroids seems to have teeth, and it's making funny noises.

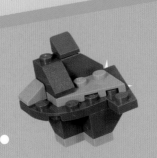

1x2 tile with bar forms a spoiler for the hoverboard

Stacked brown and tan pieces make perfect asteroids

 HOW TO BUILD!

BASE

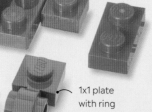

1x2 grille tile

1x2/ 1x2 inverted bracket

1x1 round plate

1x1 slope

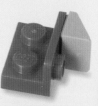

1x1 round tile with bar

1x1 plate with ring

HOVERBOARDS

On Earth, scientists are working to create real-life hoverboards using electromagnetic technology. Would you like to go to school on a hoverboard, or would you stick with the bus?

Transparent blue 1x1 round plate thrusters

WHY IS THAT ASTEROID SNARLING?

Aerodynamic pointed front

1x2 jumper plates for Kori to stand on

UH-OH...

This asteroid has a passenger. It's a space slug called an exogorth, and it's looking for some fast food! Kori may be pretty speedy on her hoverboard, but she definitely doesn't want to be lunch. Is she quick enough to give this slippery customer a swerve?

THAT'S TOO CLOSE FOR COMFORT!

Floating space debris

HOW TO BUILD!

ASTEROID

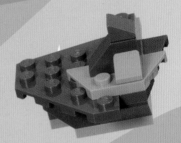

1x2 slope brick

2x4 wedge plate

4x4 wedge plate

2x4 plate

2x2 inverted slope brick

NECK

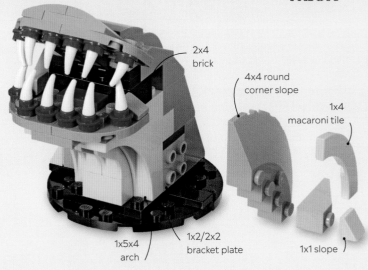

2x4 brick

4x4 round corner slope

1x4 macaroni tile

1x5x4 arch

1x2/2x2 bracket plate

1x1 slope

UPPER JAW

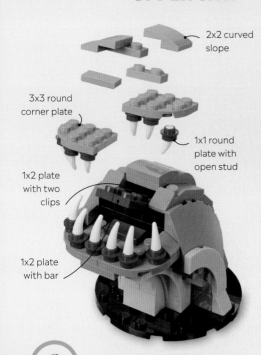

2x2 curved slope

3x3 round corner plate

1x1 round plate with open stud

1x2 plate with two clips

1x2 plate with bar

1

2

HOW TO BUILD!

SLUG SNACKS

The largest real-life slug grows up to 8 in (20 cm) long. They can eat almost anything, including plants, fungus, and worms. Luckily, they don't have enormous teeth like space slugs do!

Horn pieces create a toothy smile

Exogorth "pops" out of a hole made from black plates

SPACE SLUG GRUB

Too late! The exogorth gobbles Kori up. Ugh! It's slimy and dark in its tummy. Kori trips over some candy and bumps into a runaway stormtrooper in hiding from the Empire. What can she build to help her get out?

THE PLAN = ?

USEFUL BRICKS

L-SHAPED BAR

BAR WITH STUDS

LONG LEGO® TECHNIC PIN

OBSTACLES

CANDY

JUST CALL ME SLIMETROOPER.

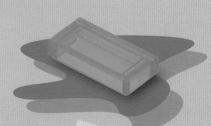

THROAT SLIME

PREVIOUS MEALS

BUILDING IDEAS

FEATHERY THROAT-TICKLER

SNEEZE-INDUCING FLOWERS

TONGUE-BURNING LIGHTSABERS

...THAT'S IT!

What a ticklish situation! That gives Kori an idea. She builds a tickler and tickles the exogorth's throat until it sneezes. Achoo! Kori hurtles out of the exogorth's mouth and lands on a passing asteroid.

Feather piece for tickling exogorth throats!

Bar with side studs allows the tickler to rotate and bend

SNEEZING

People—and animals—sneeze when something irritates the trigeminal nerve in their nose and mouth. It could be germs, pollen, dust, or a tickly feather.

I WANT TO STAY HERE WITH ALL THE CANDY!

NICE AND "SNEEZY"...

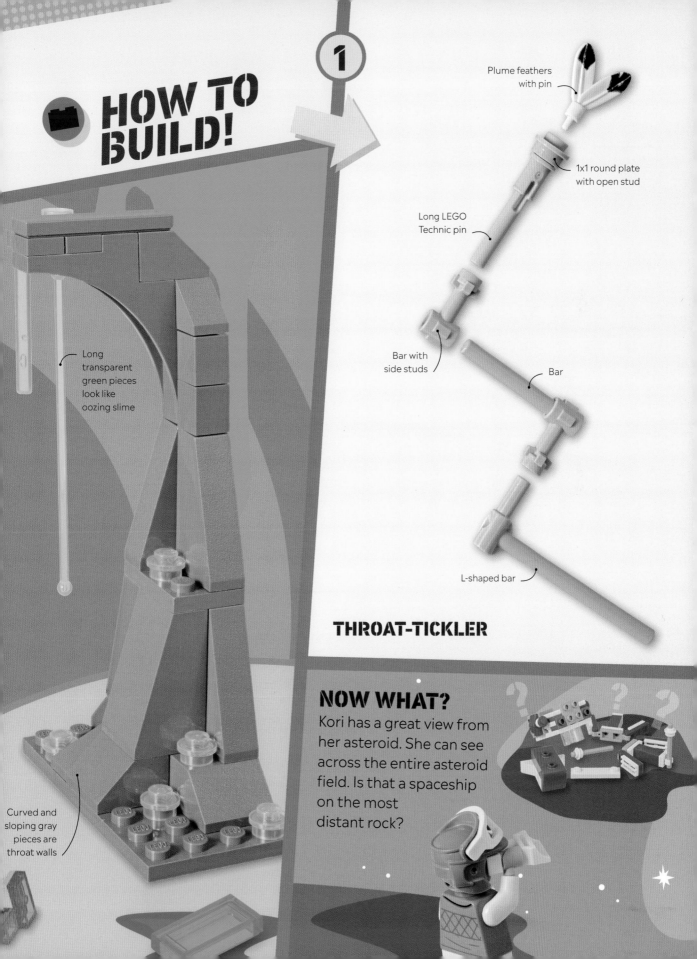

HOW TO BUILD!

Plume feathers with pin

1x1 round plate with open stud

Long LEGO Technic pin

Bar with side studs

Bar

Long transparent green pieces look like oozing slime

L-shaped bar

THROAT-TICKLER

Curved and sloping gray pieces are throat walls

NOW WHAT?

Kori has a great view from her asteroid. She can see across the entire asteroid field. Is that a spaceship on the most distant rock?

ROCK HOPPING

Yes! That's a spaceship alright. Maybe Kori could fly it home to Hoth. Now, what can she build to get her to the distant asteroid? Kori must avoid getting caught in the crossfire of two ships fighting each other nearby.

THE PLAN = ?

⚠ OBSTACLES

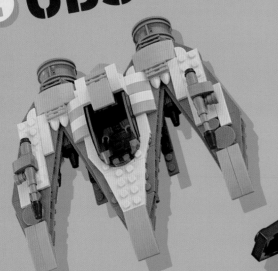

FIERCE FIGHTERS

I'LL GET THOSE ROTTEN REBELS!

USEFUL BRICKS

2X2 RADAR DISH

1X2X²/₃ BRICK WITH STUDS ON THE SIDES AND HANDLE

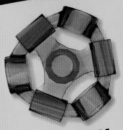

RING WITH THREE BARS

BUILDING IDEAS

GRAVITY-DEFYING CATAPULT

ASTEROID-HOOKING CRANE

POWERFUL TRACTOR BEAM

...THAT'S IT!

A tractor beam could be perfect for pulling the asteroid with the abandoned ship safely toward Kori. She builds one quickly. Kori switches it on and sees the asteroid rise and gently begin moving. Here we go! Up, up, up...

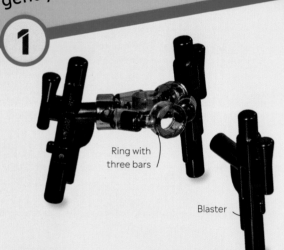

1

Ring with three bars

Blaster

BASE

2

1X2X⅔ brick with studs on the sides and handle

1x2 printed tile

1x1 round plate with hole

2x2 radar dish

Bar

DISH

HOW TO BUILD!

I WON'T BE DRAWN INTO YOUR FIGHT.

1x1 round plate with hole

Three LEGO blasters make sturdy legs

GIVE US A LIFT

Powerful tractor beams like Kori's don't exist on Earth... yet! Scientists are working to develop tractor beam technology using light and sound waves to move very tiny objects.

GET OUT OF THE WAY THEN!

Black wedge plates make TIE interceptor wings

STRAY SHOT

And down, down, down again. Kori's tractor beam is destroyed by one of the fighters. She's back to square one. Or asteroid one.

MISCHIEVOUS MYNOCKS

All that fuss has attracted some nearby Mynocks! A group of the large, winged creatures have arrived and Kori is right in the thick of it. She needs to get out of here... and fast! What should Kori build?

THE PLAN = ?

BUILDING IDEAS

FLOATING HOT-AIR BALLOON

PROPELLING ROCKET POD LAUNCHER

HOW CAN I REACH THE SHIP ON THE NEXT ASTEROID?

! OBSTACLES

INCOMING MYNOCKS

● USEFUL BRICKS

1X2 TILE WITH LEGO TECHNIC BEAM

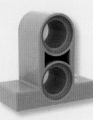

LEGO TECHNIC PIN

STURDY JETPACK

2X2 PLATE WITH PIN HOLES

...THAT'S IT!

Kori builds a powerful rocket pod launcher. She climbs onto the seat. Five, four, three, two, one... blast off! She soon touches down on the distant asteroid, close to an ARC-170 ship. It's damaged, but it looks fixable. Yay!

THIS WILL BE A BLAST!

Two levers are needed to control this rocket pod!

Rocket pod sits on a 4x8 plate with slope pieces along the edges

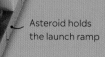

Asteroid holds the launch ramp

IT'S ROCKET SCIENCE!

It takes jet propulsion to launch a rocket. When fuel inside the rocket is ignited, it creates gases that shoot out from the back and propel the rocket forward.

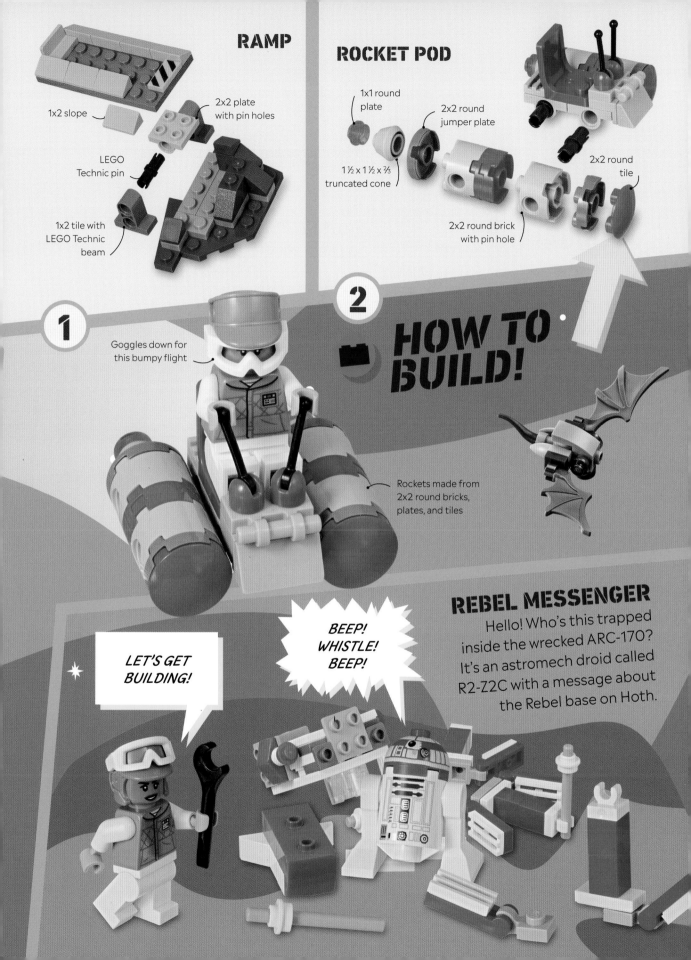

RAMP

1x2 slope

2x2 plate with pin holes

LEGO Technic pin

1x2 tile with LEGO Technic beam

ROCKET POD

1x1 round plate

1½ x 1½ x ⅔ truncated cone

2x2 round jumper plate

2x2 round tile

2x2 round brick with pin hole

1

Goggles down for this bumpy flight

2

HOW TO BUILD!

Rockets made from 2x2 round bricks, plates, and tiles

REBEL MESSENGER

Hello! Who's this trapped inside the wrecked ARC-170? It's an astromech droid called R2-Z2C with a message about the Rebel base on Hoth.

LET'S GET BUILDING!

BEEP! WHISTLE! BEEP!

TIME TO GO

The shield generator protecting the Rebel base on Hoth needs a repair, but the missing part is lost on the planet Mustafar. Kori wants to find that part. She would also like to find the instructions for fixing this ARC-170, or another way out of here!

THE PLAN = ?

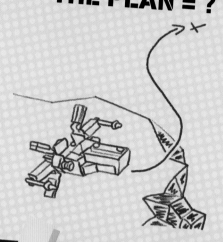

⚠ OBSTACLES

WHERE DID THOSE BUILDING INSTRUCTIONS GO?

STEP 5

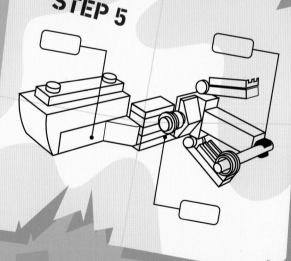

MISSING INSTRUCTIONS

1X2/2X2 BRACKET PLATE

1X1 PLATE WITH CLIP

1X2 JUMPER PLATE

1X2 PLATE WITH BAR

USEFUL BRICKS

ASTEROID SPACE BUGGY

MESSAGE-CARRYING DRONE

FIXED ARC-170

BUILDING IDEAS

...THAT'S IT!

Rebel troopers and astromechs are skilled mechanics. They're resourceful, too. After a few false starts, Kori and R2-Z2C manage to patch the ARC-170 together. The duo think their repairs will hold. Are they right?

I THINK I'VE FIGURED IT OUT...

1

1x2/2x2 bracket plate

SHIPBUILDING

Scientists on Earth build spacecraft from light but strong materials like aluminum. They just don't have access to the array of galactic metals available in the *Star Wars* world!

LEGO Technic pins add extra stability

2

WRRK-WRRK. WEEEOOP.

The ship's colors match its astromech mechanic

Bar pieces are the ship's blasters

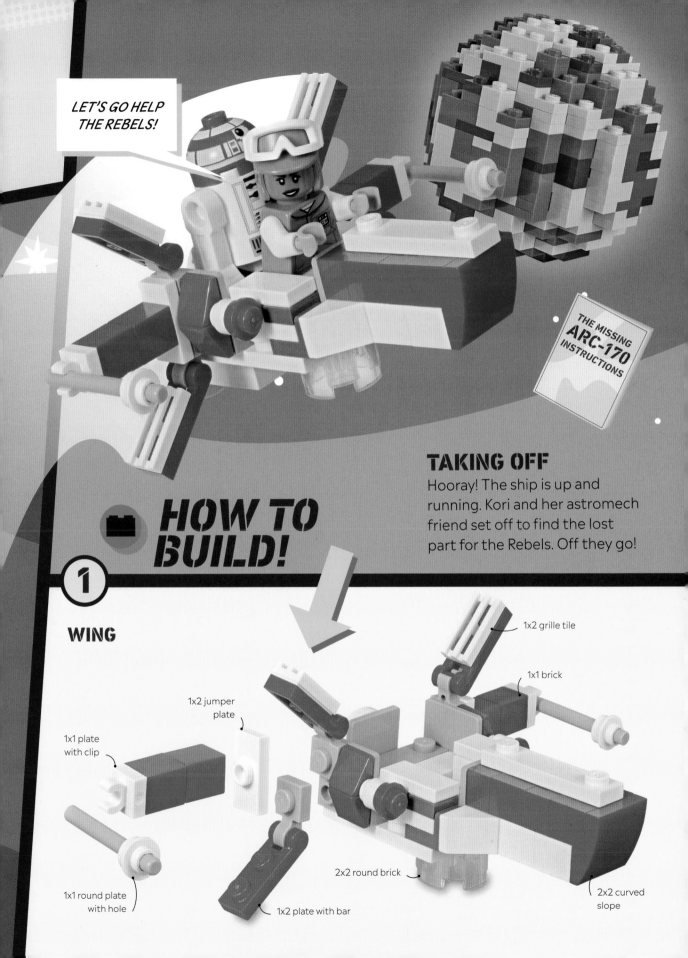

LET'S GO HELP THE REBELS!

THE MISSING **ARC-170** INSTRUCTIONS

HOW TO BUILD!

TAKING OFF

Hooray! The ship is up and running. Kori and her astromech friend set off to find the lost part for the Rebels. Off they go!

①

WING

1x2 grille tile

1x1 brick

1x2 jumper plate

1x1 plate with clip

1x1 round plate with hole

1x2 plate with bar

2x2 round brick

2x2 curved slope

DESERT WORLD

That engine sounds shaky! Kori makes an emergency stop on the desert planet of Tatooine. But Jawas from a nearby sandcrawler scurry over, hoping to grab the astromech to sell as scrap. Eek! How can Kori and her pal escape?

THE PLAN = ?

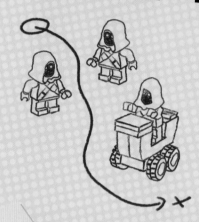

!OBSTACLES

SAVVY JAWAS

BOWA UTINNI!!

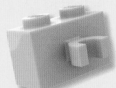

1X2 BRICK WITH CLIP

1X2 TILE

1X2 MASONRY BRICK

USEFUL BRICKS

 # BUILDING IDEAS

RIDEABLE BANTHAS

 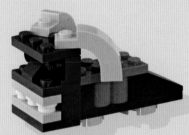

JAWA TRAP

MIND-BOGGLING MAZE

...THAT'S IT!

Kori builds a maze with twists and turns, and fills it with fake droids. The Jawas follow the decoys into the maze. Ha... fooled them! While the Jawas are stuck in the maze, Kori and her pal make a dash for it.

AMAZING MAZES

Mazes are a great puzzle for a mathematician. A difficult maze is an opportunity for problem solving, and the head-scratching puzzles have also been very important in the study of graphs.

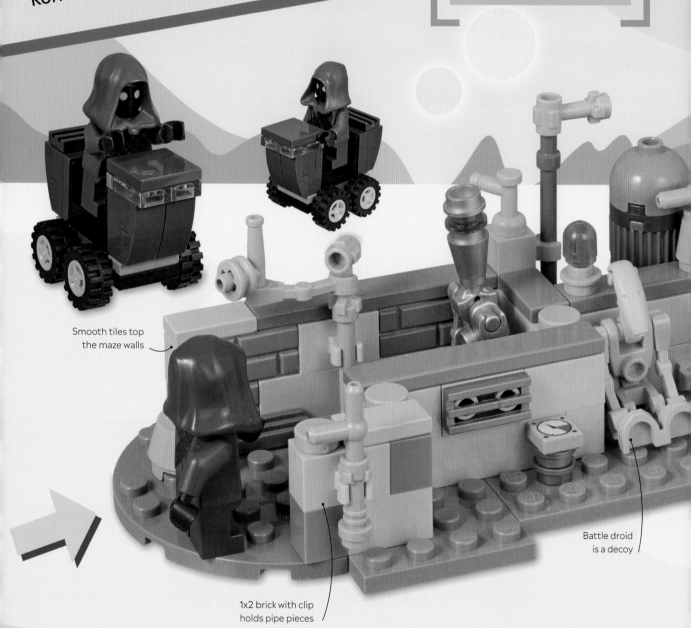

Smooth tiles top the maze walls

1x2 brick with clip holds pipe pieces

Battle droid is a decoy

2x2 truncated cone

1x1 round tile

4x8 half round plate

1x4 tile

1x2 tile

1

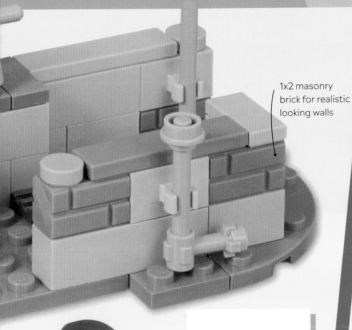

1x2 masonry brick for realistic looking walls

NEKKEL JUUVAR OBWEGADADA!

HOW TO BUILD!

INTO THE PIT

The friends run so fast that they don't watch where they are going. And that's straight into a big hole in the sand. Oof!

WATCH OUT! SARLACC PIT

DOWN IN THE PIT

Yikes! They've fallen into a sarlacc pit. The monster at the bottom looks ravenous. They can tell by its gaping jaws. Oh, this really is the pits! How can Kori and R2-Z2C stop those toothy jaws from closing on them?

THE PLAN = ?

OBSTACLES

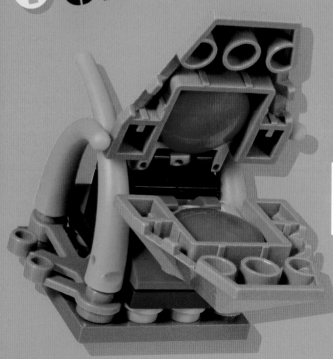

HUNGRY SARLACC

LOOKS LIKE WE HAVE TO MAKE A PIT STOP!

4X4X1⅓ PYRAMID WEDGE

1X2 PLATE WITH BAR

1X1 PLATE WITH CLIP

DINOSAUR TAIL PIECE

USEFUL BRICKS

BUILDING IDEAS

DROID DECOY

TASTY BURGERS

RAMPAGING CREATURE

...THAT'S IT!

Ah, here comes one of the droids from the maze.
Clever Kori has used her tools to reprogram it.
The droid distracts the sarlacc with tasty scraps
of Womp Rat meat while Kori and R2-Z2C
silently clamber out of the pit. Phew!

**WATCH OUT!
SARLACC PIT**

2x2 slide plate makes a
slobbery palate

Bar holder
with clip holds
Womp Rat meat

1

HEAD

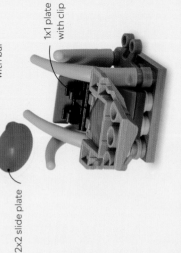

4x4x1½
pyramid wedge

1x2 plate
with bar

1x1 plate
with clip

2x2 slide plate

2

BASE

Dinosaur
tail piece

2x3 plate

1x1 round plate

3x4 plant
leaf

4x4 plate

Sarlacc pit sits
on a bed of
plants, green
plates, and slopes

HOW TO BUILD!

BACK IN THE DUNES

Outside the pit, Kori and R2-Z2C sit and think about what to do next. In the distance, they can see a small building that might be worth checking out!

WATCH OUT! SARLACC PIT

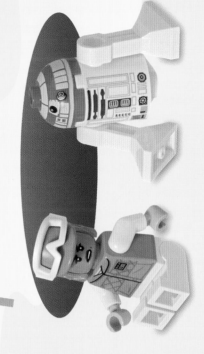

SHHH, QUIETLY DOES IT!

Wrench is useful for programming droids

WHIRRR... WHIRRR...

PIT PREDATOR

There's a real-life insect that acts a bit like a sarlacc. The antlion lives in deserts. Its larva digs a pit in the sand and waits at the bottom for passing prey to fall in.

Droid stands on a 4x4 round plate

JUNK SHOP GEM

They've found a deserted junk shop. Great! There must be odds and ends here that Kori can use for an emergency build. She has to be quick, though. The Jawas are back on the trail, and a Tusken Raider is hanging around outside.

THE PLAN = ?

⚠ OBSTACLES

SCAVENGING JAWAS

LOCAL RAIDERS

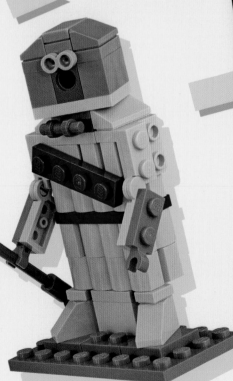

BUILDING IDEAS

SPEEDY PODRACER

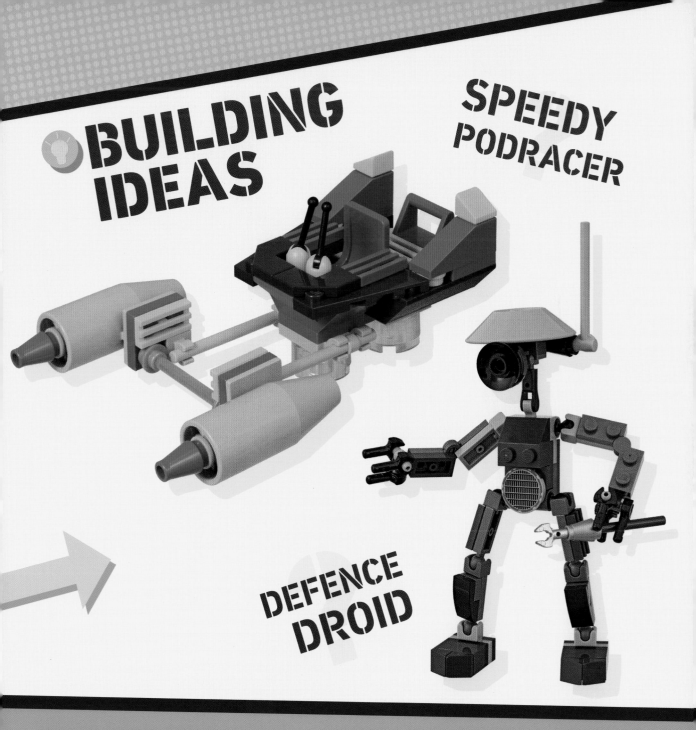

DEFENCE DROID

USEFUL BRICKS

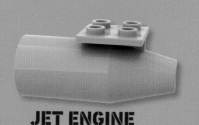

JET ENGINE

1X1 CONE

1X3 SLOPE

4X6 DOUBLE INVERTED SLOPE

...THAT'S IT!

Using parts from the junk shop, Kori builds a podracer. She and the astromech climb in and zip away. Wheee... this is fast. It's really fast. It's too fast! The podracer is out of control and heading for a crash.

Messy junk shop floor!

HOW TO BUILD!

1

WALLS

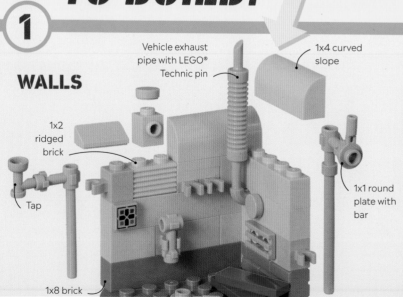

Vehicle exhaust pipe with LEGO® Technic pin

1x4 curved slope

1x2 ridged brick

Tap

1x1 round plate with bar

1x8 brick

2

TABLE

1x1 cone

1x1 round plate with hole

1x1 round brick

ENGINE

1x1 cone

1x2 grille tile

1x1 plate with clip

Bar with stopper

Jet engine piece

POD

2x2 driving seat

1x3 slope

Lever

2x2 corner tile

4x6 double inverted slope

2

1

HOW TO BUILD!

DOH... I FORGOT THE BRAKES!

Slope pieces shape the front of the pod

PODRACERS

In the *Star Wars* galaxy, podracers travel at speeds of up to 500 miles per hour (800 kilometers per hour). That's more than twice as fast as a Formula 1 racing car.

Powerful gray podracer engines

CANTINA CRASH...

Bang! The podracer crashes right outside the Mos Eisley cantina. Kori jumps to her feet and checks the astromech. It's fine. So is she, but she is pretty thirsty. Let's see what this lively cantina has to offer.

GET READY FOR A BUMPY LANDING!

Large, thick wheels for driving across the desert

Transparent plates are sandcrawler windows

Orange bar is energy binder arc

HOW TO BUILD!

①

2x2 tile

1x2 plate

1x2 grille tile

1x2 curved slope

2x2 plate

2x2x⅔ plate with side studs

SANDCRAWLER

②

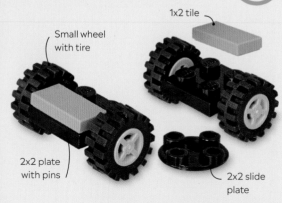

1x2 tile

Small wheel with tire

2x2 plate with pins

2x2 slide plate

WHEELS

THIRST QUENCHERS

Jabba juice, blue milk, and Hutt's Delight are on the menu at the Mos Eisley cantina. Earth astronauts can only have tea, coffee, fruit juice, or water!

The amazing Modal Nodes
[PLAYING TODAY!]

I HAVE A VERY NICE SHIP FOR SALE...

Bottles decorate the cantina

A BANTHA MILKSHAKE?

2x2 round ridged brick for table legs

Cup holds delicious Jabba juice!

49

SHIP FOR SALE

The cantina patrons are friendly. It's the noisy sandtroopers arriving who are the problem. Gulp! Kori must find a way out of here and on to Mustafar pronto. Hey, did someone just mention a bounty hunter ship for sale?

THE PLAN = ?

⚠ OBSTACLES

CANTINA PATRONS

LOUD SANDTROOPERS

USEFUL BRICKS

3X3 ROUND CORNER PLATE

1X1 BRICK WITH SIDE STUD

3X6 WEDGE PLATE

2X2 CURVED SLOPE

I'M SURE THEY WON'T MIND IF I BORROW IT.

BUILDING IDEAS

WALKING DANCETRON

SPEEDY ROLLER BLADES

SNEAKY BOUNTY HUNTER SHIP

...THAT'S IT!

Kori goes to the dock to speak to the seller. She easily repairs the old bounty hunter ship, and off they blast. That's when the troopers suddenly notice them. Nobody told Kori that the ship's last owner was wanted by the Empire!

BOUNTY HUNTERS

A bounty hunter is someone who captures fugitives in return for payment. In the *Star Wars* galaxy, bounty hunters pilot ships of all shapes and sizes.

WARNING DOCKYARD AHEAD

1x4x5 panel with window makes walls

Printed tile is a control panel

FRONT

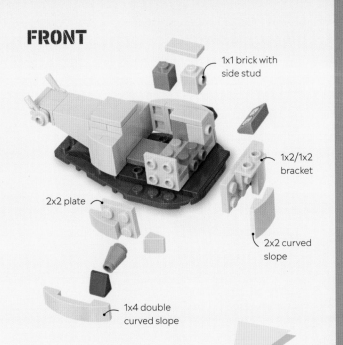

1x1 brick with side stud

1x2/1x2 bracket

2x2 plate

2x2 curved slope

1x4 double curved slope

BASE

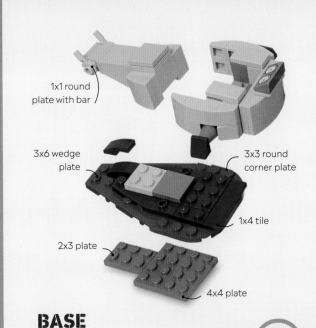

1x1 round plate with bar

3x6 wedge plate

3x3 round corner plate

1x4 tile

2x3 plate

4x4 plate

①

HOW TO BUILD!

FOLLOW THAT BOUNTY HUNTER!

LET ME JUST GRAB THE KEYS FOR YOU.

②

HEAD FIRST INTO ACTION

Can the duo shake off their Imperial pursuers? Full throttle and go!

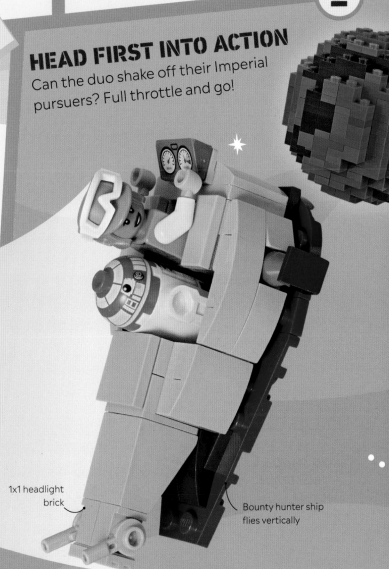

1x1 headlight brick

Bounty hunter ship flies vertically

TIE PURSUIT

The Imperials in their TIE interceptors are catching up fast. What to do? Kori looks down and sees a planet. It isn't Mustafar, but it will do. She decides to abandon ship, but now she needs to build some kind of landing craft, and fast!

THE PLAN = ?

⚠ OBSTACLES

I DON'T WANT TO GET "TIE-D" UP IN THIS MESS!

ANGRY TIE INTERCEPTORS

2X2X2 STAND WITH HOLE

3X3 WEDGE PLATE

HANDLEBARS

4X4 ROUND CORNER PLATE

USEFUL BRICKS

BUILDING IDEAS

BUCKET ZIPLINE

HANDY HOVERCOPTER

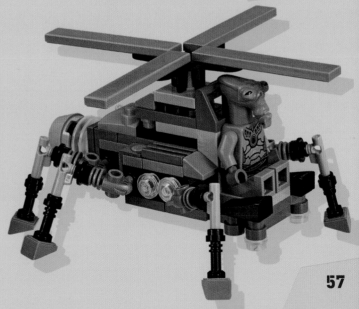

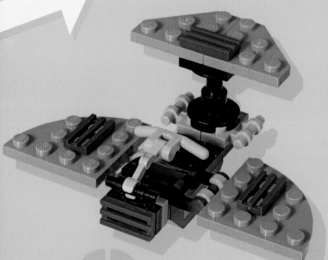

GENTLE GLIDER

TAIL AND WING

- 3x3 wedge plate
- 2x2x2 stand with hole
- 1x2 plate with handle
- 1x2 plate with bar
- Handlebars
- 1x2 plate with two clips
- 4x4 round corner plate

HOW TO BUILD!

...THAT'S IT!

Kori builds a glider and cruises with R2-Z2C down toward the strange planet of Dagobah. Seconds later, a TIE interceptor blows the bounty hunter ship to bits above them. Crumbs... that was close!

EW... LOOKS SWAMPY DOWN THERE.

- Tailfin keeps the glider balanced
- Glider wings can move up and down

GLIDERS

A glider is a plane without an engine. Real-life gliders use warm air currents to stay up, because warm air rises. Unlike Kori's glider, they must be towed into the air to begin their flight.

STUCK IN A TREE

Oof! The duo land in a tree. They can't climb down because the tree is in a sticky swamp. But there's another tree growing nearby on dry land. Hmm...

AIM FOR THE TREES!

IIII...ZZZZ...

Kori holds on tight to the handlebars!

SWAMPY SHORES

The tree is getting less comfy by the minute. Kori has twigs in her pants, and R2-Z2C has leaves in its gears. Time to get moving! But what can they build to get them off the swamp tree and onto dry land?

THE PLAN = ?

⊙ OBSTACLES

> *I THINK WE'D BETTER "LEAF"!*

POISONOUS PLANTS

USEFUL BRICKS

1X4X5 ARCH

2X2X2 SLOPE BRICK

1X1 PLATE WITH CLIP

BAR LADDER WITH CLIPS

BUILDING IDEAS

FLOATING RAFT

FLYING BOGWING

TREE-TO-TREE MONKEY BARS

61

...THAT'S IT!

There's no time to hang about. Kori builds some monkey bars and grabs R2-Z2C. Then they swing across to the next tree and jump lightly to the ground. Ta-da! Aren't they clever?

SQUELCHY SWAMPS

On Earth, swamps form where soil does not drain well and water gathers. They are home to frogs, fish, and alligators, but luckily none of the unusual Dagobah creatures.

MONKEY BARS

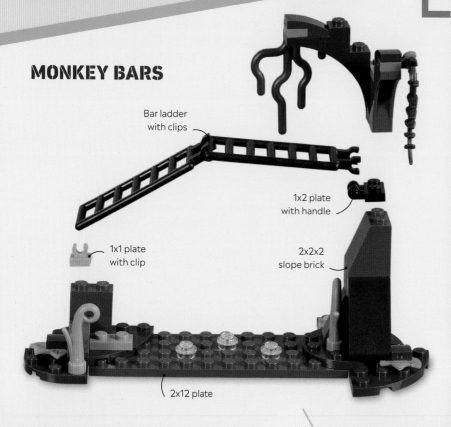

Bar ladder with clips

1x2 plate with handle

1x1 plate with clip

2x2x2 slope brick

2x12 plate

Dagobah is full of green swamp plants!

HOW TO BUILD!

62

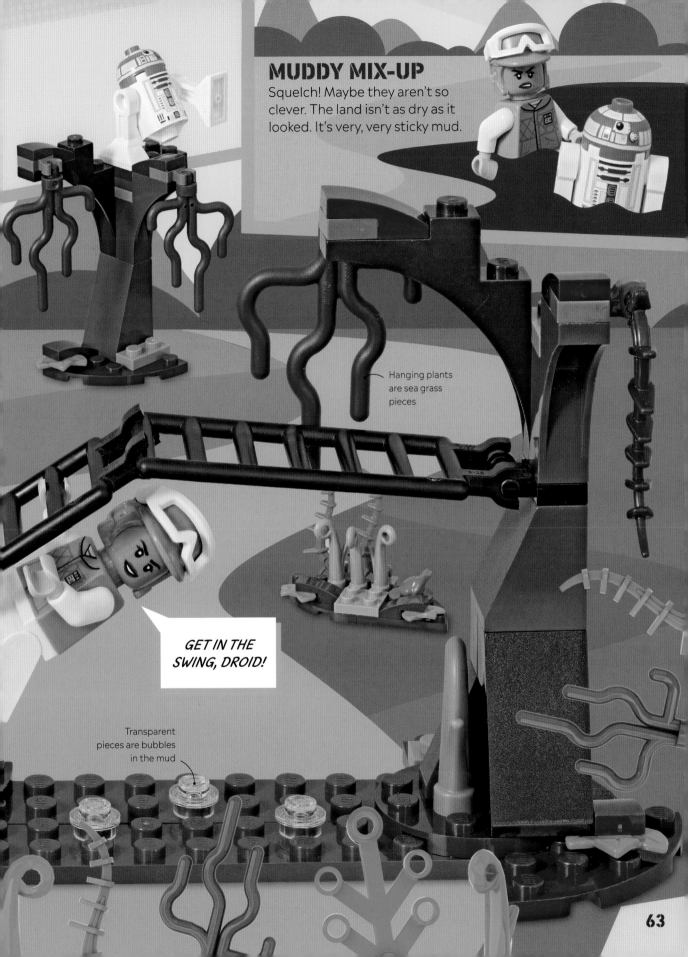

MUDDY MIX-UP

Squelch! Maybe they aren't so clever. The land isn't as dry as it looked. It's very, very sticky mud.

Hanging plants are sea grass pieces

GET IN THE SWING, DROID!

Transparent pieces are bubbles in the mud

STICKY SITUATION

R2-Z2C and Kori are stuck in the mud... very sticky mud! She tries to take a step, but she's caught in the swamp's muck and slime. Kori needs to get out of here fast. How will she get across the boggy ground without sinking?

THE PLAN = ?

! OBSTACLES

MURKY MUD

SWAMP SLIME

INQUISITIVE JEDI MASTER

64

USEFUL BRICKS

1X2 PLATE WITH BALL

2X2 AIR SCOOP ENGINE

1X2 PLATE WITH BALL AND SOCKET

2X2 INVERTED CURVED SLOPE

> BRRR..ZZ... EEP!

BUILDING IDEAS

SWAMP SKIS

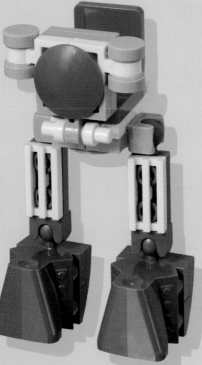

TALL MECH SUIT

COMFY SEDAN CHAIR

...THAT'S IT!

A strong mech suit is perfect for stepping over sticky mud and bog slime. It also can outrun Master Yoda, who has invited Kori to his hut for dinner. Yoda persuades R2-Z2C to stay, but Kori wants to rush back to base.

ROOT LEAF STEW? ER... NO, THANKS!

MECHANICAL EXOSUITS

These special suits have mechanical parts that act like human muscles. Some exosuits can walk, pick up objects, and help humans with jobs.

1x2 grille tile looks like vents

Useful handlebars control the mech

Heavy feet can walk through slime and keep the mech balanced

HOW TO BUILD!

1

1x1 round tile

1x1 plate with clip

2x2 driving seat

2x2 slide plate

1x2 plate with clip

SEAT

2

LEG

1x2 plate with ball socket

1x2 plate with ball and socket

2x2 air scoop engine

1x2 plate with ball in the middle

2x2 inverted curved slope

HAVE MANY VISITORS, I DO NOT.

Space on the back of mech to add extra equipment

Ball and socket connections mean feet and legs can move

WIGGLY ROOTS

The mech steps on something in the mud. Is it a tree root? No, tree roots don't hiss and wriggle, or have huge fangs!

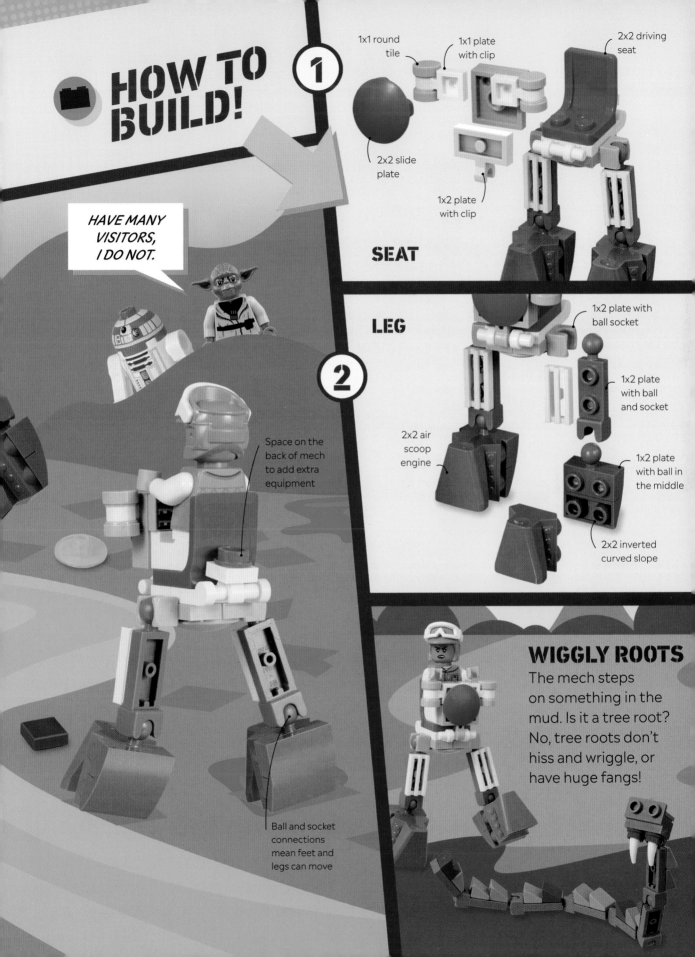

DRAGONSNAKE DANGER

It's a dragonsnake! The giant reptile rears up and... crunch! The mech suit is crushed like a tin can. Kori squeezes free, but the predator still has its sights on her. She'll have to quickly build another way out of this swamp.

THE PLAN = ?

OBSTACLES

"FANGS" FOR NOTHING!

WILD DRAGONSNAKE

USEFUL BRICKS

1X4 BRICK WITH 3 HOLES

1X2/1X2 INVERTED BRACKET

1X3 CURVED SLOPE

1X2 PLATE WITH HANDLE

PROPELLER

BUILDING IDEAS

DISTRACTING KYBER CRYSTAL

SPEEDY SUBMARINE

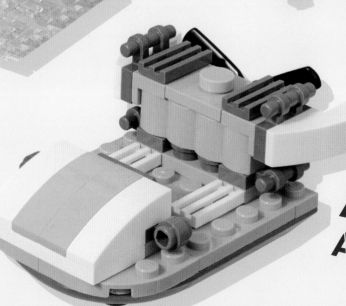

AGILE AIRBOAT

69

...THAT'S IT!

An airboat is perfect for this trip. It whooshes across the bog, fast as the wind. Wheeeee! Bye-bye, dragonsnake. And oh... hello Rebels! Kori's comms unit splutters into life. It's working again. Thank goodness!

Bright 1x3 curved slopes make the boat's bow

HISSSSS!

SORRY... CAN'T STICK AROUND.

Colorful spines on dragonsnake's back

1x1 slope

1x2 plate with ball and socket

1x2 plate with socket

DRAGONSNAKE

Horn piece

Front of the airboat is curved

HOW TO BUILD!

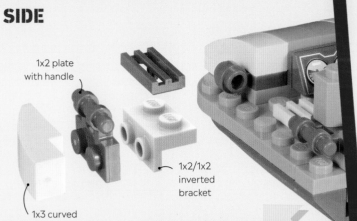

1x2 plate with handle

1x2/1x2 inverted bracket

1x3 curved slope

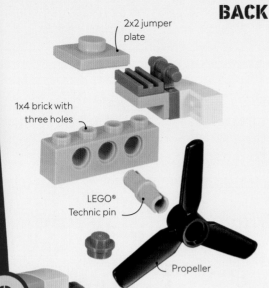

2x2 jumper plate

1x4 brick with three holes

LEGO® Technic pin

Propeller

HOW TO BUILD!

① ②

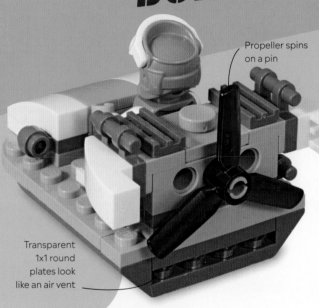

Propeller spins on a pin

Transparent 1x1 round plates look like an air vent

URGENT MESSAGE

A message from Hoth comes over the comms unit...

GET TO MUSTAFAR NOW. OUR SHIELD GENERATOR IS ON ITS LAST LEGS!

AIRBOATS

Airboats are ideal for shallow waters, where there is no room for an underwater propeller. These flat-bottomed craft have their propellers at the back, above the water's surface.

Studs on the inverted bracket are dragonsnake eyes

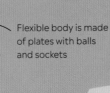

Flexible body is made of plates with balls and sockets

NO TIME FOR STEW

Kori had best get building, but she's on her own because R2-Z2C is off to have dinner with Yoda. The Jedi Master insists that Kori join them, but there is no time. However tempting the opportunity is! She must get to Mustafar.

THE PLAN = ?

! OBSTACLES

BUT A SPECIALITY MY ROOT LEAF STEW IS!

MYSTERY STEW

2X2 DOME

2X2 ROUND PLATE

AXLE CONNECTOR

AXLE WITH STUD

AXLE WITH REVERSER HANDLE

USEFUL BRICKS

BUILDING IDEAS

CLASSIC Y-WING

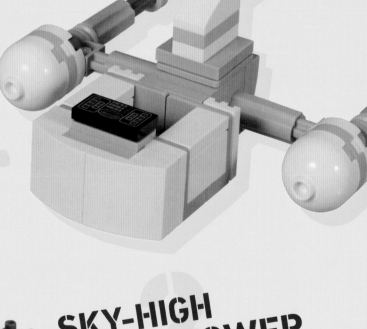

SKY-HIGH EWOK TOWER

...THAT'S IT!

A Y-wing seems the best option. Well, why not? Kori builds a microfighter Y-wing and takes off for Mustafar. The microfighter is fun to fly, but there's no time for aerobatics. Kori's got places to go and parts to find!

XS AND YS

The creator of *Star Wars*, George Lucas, took inspiration from real-world fighter planes. Y-wings and X-wings are fast and powerful, making them great for dogfights.

1

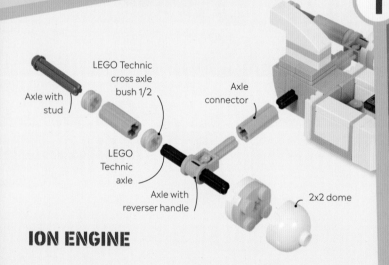

Axle with stud

LEGO Technic cross axle bush 1/2

Axle connector

LEGO Technic axle

Axle with reverser handle

2x2 dome

ION ENGINE

2

BACK

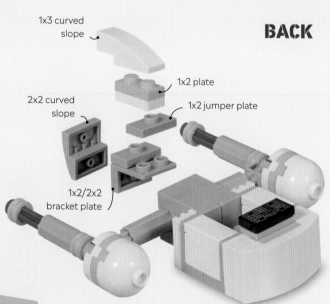

1x3 curved slope

1x2 plate

2x2 curved slope

1x2 jumper plate

1x2/2x2 bracket plate

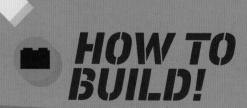

HOW TO BUILD!

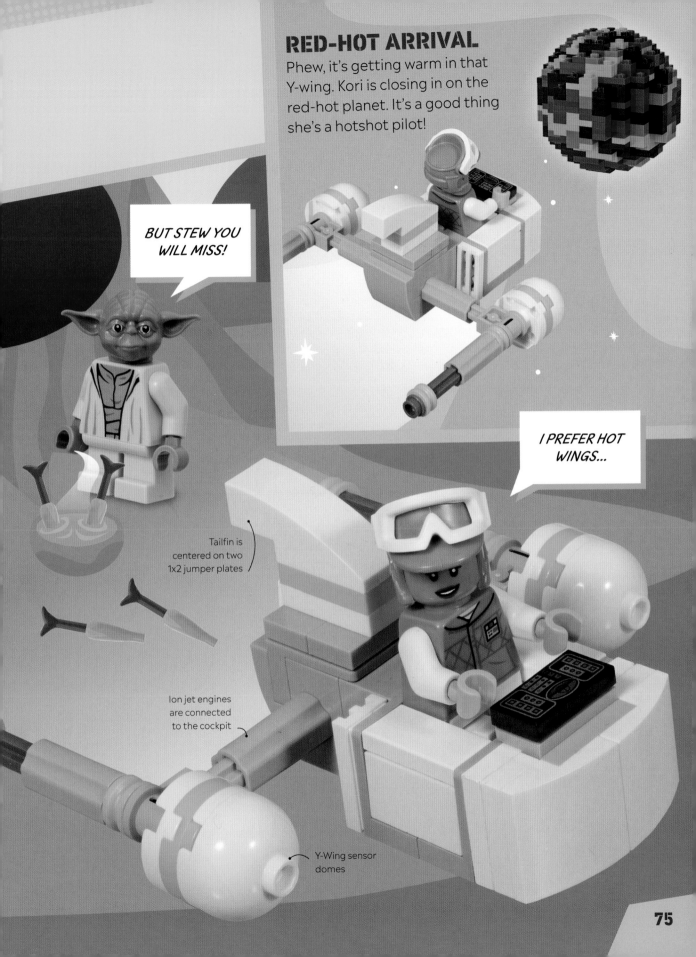

RED-HOT ARRIVAL

Phew, it's getting warm in that Y-wing. Kori is closing in on the red-hot planet. It's a good thing she's a hotshot pilot!

BUT STEW YOU WILL MISS!

I PREFER HOT WINGS...

Tailfin is centered on two 1x2 jumper plates

Ion jet engines are connected to the cockpit

Y-Wing sensor domes

SKIFF SAILING

Kori lands the Y-wing on Mustafar and calls the Rebels on Hoth to ask about the missing part. Oh no! It's on the far side of a boiling lava lake. Imperial mouse droids patrol the banks, so Kori has no choice but to cross the hot lava. What will she build?

THE PLAN = ?

! OBSTACLES

WATCHFUL MOUSE DROIDS

RED-HOT LAVA

1X2 CURVED SLOPE

1X4 TILE

1X2/1X2 INVERTED BRACKET

1½X2X2 PLATE WITH LADDER

1X2 INVERTED SLOPE

 **USEFUL BRICKS**

 BUILDING IDEAS

LAVA-MOPPING DROID

FLOATING LAVA SKIFF

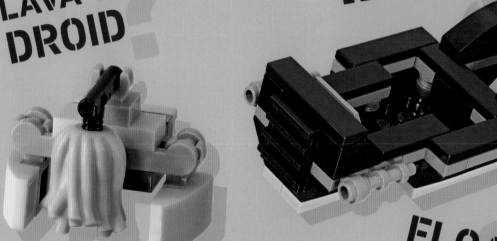

IMPERIAL WATER SCOOTER

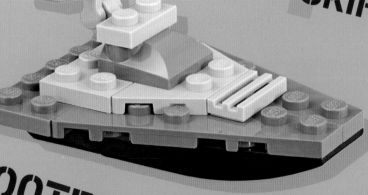

...THAT'S IT!

A skiff is perfect to whisk Kori over the bubbling lake. Wow, this is smooth sailing! She only wishes she had a telescope, like a real ship's captain. It would help her spot the missing part she's looking for.

LAVA

Hot, liquid rock that bubbles away beneath a planet's surface is known as magma. When the surface cracks and the magma flows up and out, it is called lava.

THIS SKIFF IS HOT STUFF!

Imperial colors help Kori blend in with Imperial ships

Black slopes look like jagged lava rocks

Yellow plates are the model base

HOW TO BUILD!

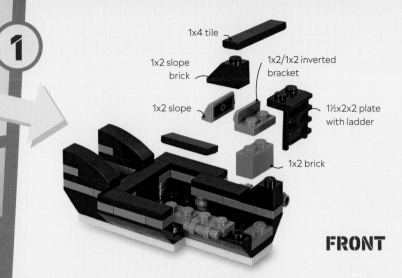

1

- 1x4 tile
- 1x2 slope brick
- 1x2/1x2 inverted bracket
- 1x2 slope
- 1½x2x2 plate with ladder
- 1x2 brick

FRONT

2

- 1x4 tile
- 2x2 corner plate
- 1x2 inverted slope
- 1x1 brick
- 1x6 plate
- 1x8 plate

BACK AND BASE

Engine vent doubles as a ladder

ON DRY LAND

Land ahoy! Kori is very glad to jump off the skiff now. Her feet are starting to feel a bit warm.

FIERY ENEMIES

Kori jumps off the lava skiff just in time. No wonder her feet were hot. The skiff is melting! Kori is happy to be on dry land as the skiff sinks. She isn't so happy when an Imperial shuttle lands near her. What can she build to throw the troopers off?

THE PLAN = ?

! OBSTACLES

PATROL SHUTTLE !

STORMTROOPERS ON THE MOVE !

HEY YOU! WHAT ARE YOU DOING HERE?

USEFUL BRICKS

ROUND CONNECTOR WITH SLOT

LEGO® TECHNIC PIN

HALF PIN

1X2 BRICK WITH TWO HOLES

1X1 MACARONI TUBE

CHAINSAW

BUILDING IDEAS

MINING-INSPIRED
OBSTACLE COURSE

DELICIOUS MILKSHAKES

...THAT'S IT!

Kori dashes through a nearby mining complex, building an obstacle course as she goes. The Imperials chasing her must avoid a flame, dodge robot arms, and duck under steam pipes. That'll slow them down!

HOW TO BUILD!

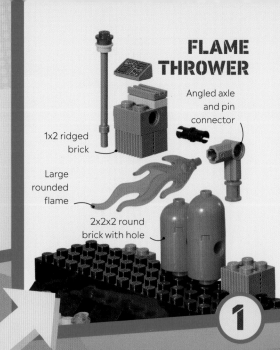

FLAME THROWER

Angled axle and pin connector

1x2 ridged brick

Large rounded flame

2x2x2 round brick with hole

1

Robot arms made from connected silver pieces

Transparent flame piece fits into connector

STOP, YOU ROTTEN REBEL!

Black bricks look like a conveyor belt

MINING

On Earth, people dig mines to extract valuable materials such as coal or diamonds. It's no use looking for phrik, tibanna gas, or doonium. They are all unique to the *Star Wars* galaxy!

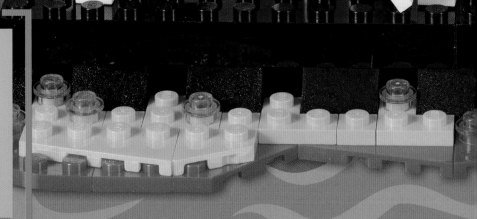

ROBOT ARMS

Space ray gun

Lightsaber hilt

Chainsaw

1x4 offset plate

2x2 dome

2x2 brick

STEAM PIPES

1x1 macaroni tube

LEGO Technic pin

Half pin

Round connector with slot

1x2x2 brick

2

3

MYSTERY FIGURE

Kori sees the missing part, but someone else is heading for it, too. Are they friend or foe?

CATCH ME IF YOU CAN!

Red tubes are hot steam pipes

Red, yellow, and orange pieces make lava

OLD FRIENDS

Kori is thrilled to find fellow Rebel Trooper Oren. It's good to see an old friend! They put their heads together and discuss builds to help them grab the part from the lava's edge. The pair need to watch out for the lava river's slippery banks!

THE PLAN = ?

! OBSTACLES

I DON'T "LAVA" THE LOOK OF THIS...

STEEP LAVA RIVER BANK

OOZING LAVA

USEFUL BRICKS

1X3 JUMPER PLATE WITH TWO STUDS

BAR WITH BALL

BAR HOLDER WITH CLIP

2X2 PLATE WITH PINS

1X2 PLATE WITH BALL AND SOCKET

BUILDING IDEAS

HEATPROOF MINING VEHICLE

WELL-TRAINED LOTH CAT

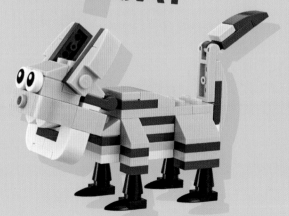

MINING DROID

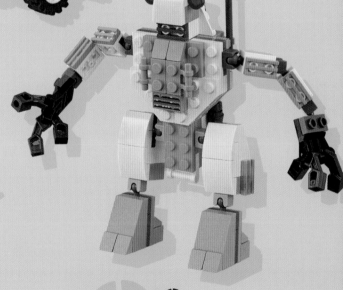

...THAT'S IT!

The friends build a mining vehicle with tough wheels. It's perfect for going over the uneven terrain. Oren stands guard and keeps an eye out for enemies, while Kori hops in the vehicle. She uses the grabbing arms to scoop up the part!

ROBOTIC ARMS

In real life, robotic arms can help with space exploration. NASA's Perseverance Mars rover has a robotic arm that can use tools.

WHAT'S THAT STRANGE CLOUD?

Grabbing arms have movable joints

HOW TO BUILD!

1

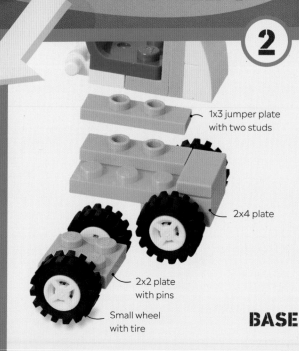

1x2 grille tile

Bar holder with clip

1x2 plate with ball and socket

Bar with ball

ARMS

2

1x3 jumper plate with two studs

2x4 plate

2x2 plate with pins

Small wheel with tire

BASE

Bar holder
with clip is
grabbing arm

TOXIC FUMES

Oren spots a cloud of volcanic gases! The pair have got the part they came for. Now they must go back across the lava.

HOW DOES THIS GRAB YOU?

Trailers can attach to 1x2 plate with handle at the back

Rebels' missing piece!

CROSSING THE LAVA

Now to get back to the Y-wing. That means crossing the lava lake again. Kori refuses to go by boat. The last one melted! Oren is nervous about the approaching volcano gases. What can the Rebels build to safely and quickly cross the lava?

THE PLAN = ?

⚠ OBSTACLES

TOXIC VOLCANIC GASES

FIERY LAVA PLUMES

2X2X10 TRIANGULAR GIRDER

1X2 INVERTED SLOPE

2X2 ROUND TILE WITH HOLE

2X2 ROUND BRICK WITH AXLE HOLE

LEGO TECHNIC AXLE PIN

USEFUL BRICKS

BUILDING IDEAS

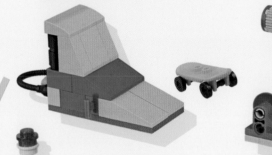

FAN AIRBOAT

TALL SKATE RAMP

I DON'T LIKE THE LOOK OF THOSE PLUMES!

ELEVATED MONORAIL

...THAT'S IT!

How about a monorail? If they build the columns tall enough, they can travel high above the dangerous lava and fumes. It's a great idea! The two Rebels high-five each other, then they get building. The stormtroopers are arriving!

FOLLOW THOSE REBELS!

IS THIS "RAILY" A GOOD IDEA, KORI?

Two girder pieces connect to make a monorail track

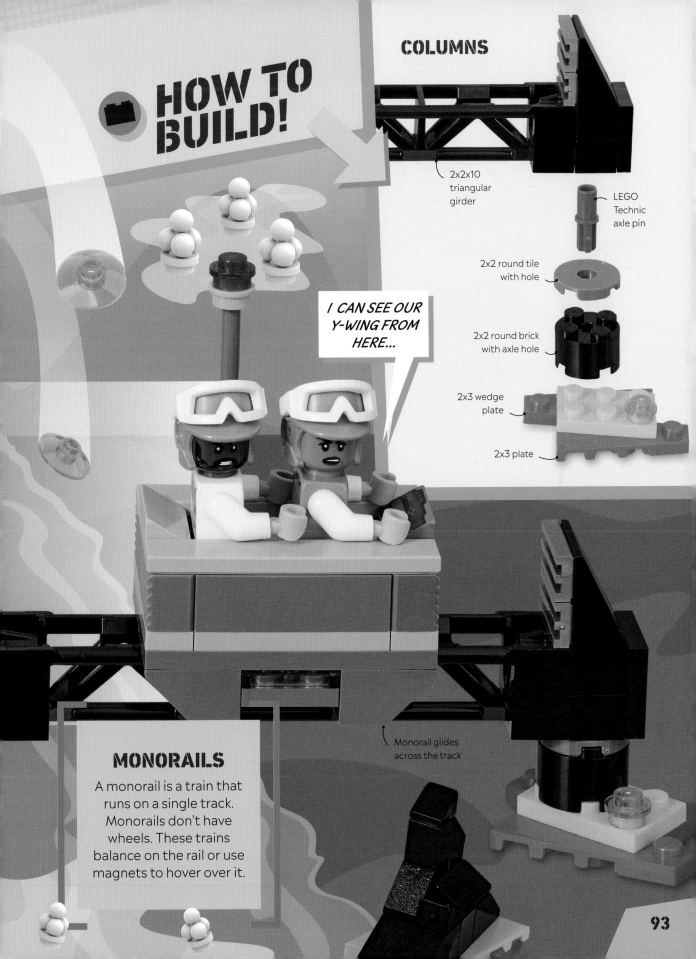

HOW TO BUILD!

COLUMNS

2x2x10 triangular girder

LEGO Technic axle pin

2x2 round tile with hole

2x2 round brick with axle hole

2x3 wedge plate

2x3 plate

I CAN SEE OUR Y-WING FROM HERE...

Monorail glides across the track

MONORAILS

A monorail is a train that runs on a single track. Monorails don't have wheels. These trains balance on the rail or use magnets to hover over it.

ON DRY LAND...

Made it! Now to find the Y-wing and fly on to Hoth. But when the Rebel Troopers hop off the monorail, their hearts sink. Their ship has been hit by a rock from a nearby erupting volcano. Oh, bubbling, boiling, bother!

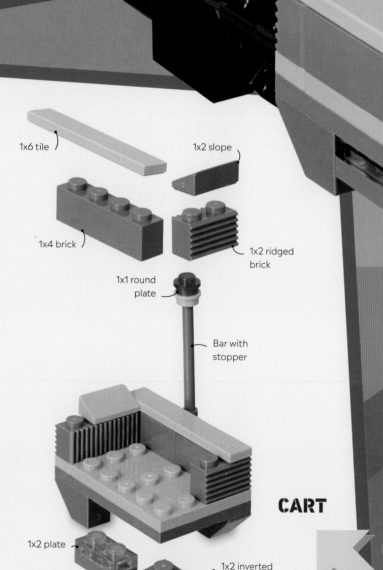

1x6 tile

1x2 slope

1x4 brick

1x2 ridged brick

1x1 round plate

Bar with stopper

2x3 inverted slope connects track and columns

CART

1x2 plate

1x2 inverted slope

HOW TO BUILD!

VOLCANIC ERUPTIONS

Like on Mustafar, when a volcano erupts on Earth it spews out lava. Eruptions also blast out rocks, gas, and lava bombs—blobs of lava which harden in midair to form rocks.

THINGS ARE STARTING TO HEAT UP!

LET'S FIND ANOTHER WAY OUT.

Damaged Y-wing can't leave Mustafar

A LOT TO DO

The Y-wing is broken, the stormtroopers are chasing, and now Kori's comms unit is pinging. Hmm. What should she attend to first?

GREAT ESCAPE

The comms unit starts up. It's Hoth base, telling Kori and Oren to get a move on. They'd love to, but there's an angry stormtrooper blocking the exit. Woah! It will take a clever build to get out of this fix and get off this planet.

THE PLAN = ?

! OBSTACLES

VOLCANIC ROCKS

ANGRY STORMTROOPER

THERE'S NO WAY OUT FOR YOU NOW.

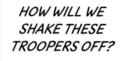

HOW WILL WE SHAKE THESE TROOPERS OFF?

USEFUL BRICKS

4X4 DOUBLE INVERTED SLOPE WITH CUTOUT

2X4 TRIPLE WEDGE

3X6 WEDGE PLATE

1X4 PLATE WITH TWO STUDS

LEGO TECHNIC BALL

BUILDING IDEAS

QUICK-FLYING BLIMP

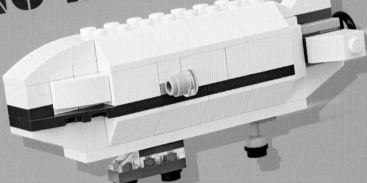

STOLEN IMPERIAL SHIP

TEMPTING LUNCH

...THAT'S IT!

The Rebel Troopers build an Imperial Star Destroyer to sneakily escape in. The enemy troopers happily wave the ship off, thinking Kori and Oren are fellow Imperials setting out on a mission. And they're away...

HOW TO BUILD!

SEE YOU LATER!

Wedge plates form the wings

THOSE STORMTROOPERS ARE DRESSED ODDLY...

Kori's sunken lava skiff

CONTROL DECKS

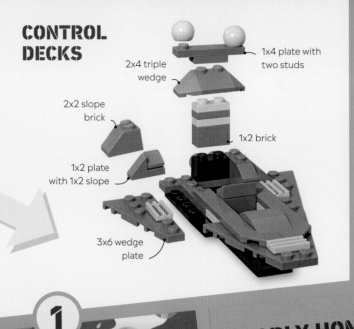

2x4 triple wedge

1x4 plate with two studs

2x2 slope brick

1x2 brick

1x2 plate with 1x2 slope

3x6 wedge plate

REAR VIEW

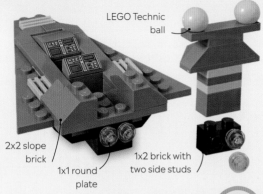

LEGO Technic ball

2x2 slope brick

1x1 round plate

1x2 brick with two side studs

②

①

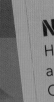

NEARLY HOME

Hooray! Snowy Hoth is in sight, and there's the Rebel base! Oren and Kori hope everyone will be happy to see them.

Pointed front of ship is aerodynamic

Printed slope bricks look like control panels

ICE PLANET

There's an ice planet in our own galaxy that's a bit like Hoth. Its name is OGLE-2005-BLG-390. Scientists don't think any tauntauns, wampas, or Rebels are living there!

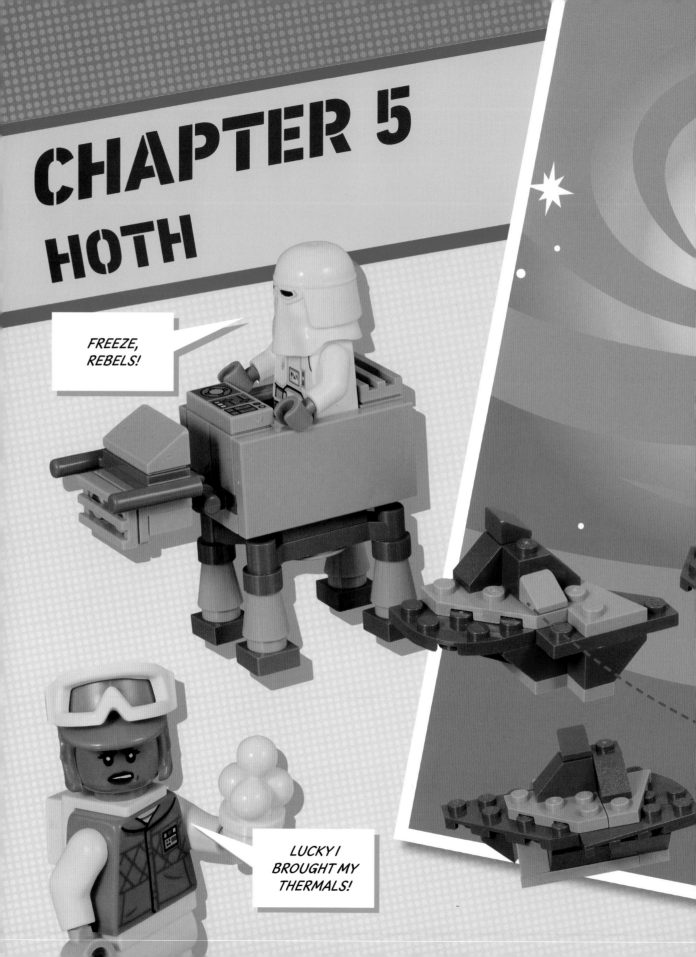

LANDING ON HOTH

The Rebels on Hoth don't know the arriving Imperial ship is being piloted by Kori and Oren, and fire at it! Kori tries to radio them, but it's too late. The ship is damaged and coming down fast. Where can Kori and Oren land safely below?

THE PLAN = ?

! OBSTACLES

SNOWTROOPER SKI TRIP

"SKI" YA LATER!

ICY SNOW CREATURE

4X4X²/₃ TRIPLE CURVED WEDGE

FOUR-SCOOP ICE-CREAM PIECE

4X8 HALF ROUND PLATE

1X3 SLOPE

1X1 VERTICAL TOOTH PLATE

USEFUL BRICKS

BUILDING IDEAS

BUBBLY HOT TUB

SOFT SNOWDRIFT

...THAT'S IT!

The Hoth Rebels build a fluffy snowdrift to soften the impact of the crash. Perfect! But those aren't Rebels waiting to greet Kori and Oren. It seems they've crashed bang in the middle of a snowtrooper ski trip.

SNOWFALL

Snow is created when water vapor high in the clouds freezes. It forms tiny ice crystals that clump together as snowflakes and fall to the ground.

I WISH I'D STAYED ON MUSTAFAR!

KEEP COOL, BUDDY.

Imperial ship fits into slot in the snowdrift

Neck bracket and 1x1 tile is toasty heat pack

TIME TO PUT OUR HEAT PACKS ON!

Stacked white slopes and bricks are pile of snow

Four-scoop ice-cream piece

ALTERNATIVE VIEW

4x4x⅔ triple curved wedge

1x1 vertical tooth plate

4x8 half round plate

1x3 slope

1x1 quarter tile piece

6x6 cut corner wedge plate

HOW TO BUILD!

GET READY!

Will the snowtroopers just melt away? No such luck. Kori can see them signaling for backup. But she won't back down.

Arms are brown carrot top pieces

Transparent blue bar is icicle

105

AT-AT ATTACK

It doesn't take long for Imperial backup to arrive. A giant metal AT-AT walker comes striding over the horizon, shooting at Kori and Oren. Gulp! They need to stop that walker in its tracks. Time to start building.

THE PLAN = ?

! OBSTACLES

I DON'T KNOW THE "FROST" THING ABOUT SNOWBALL FIGHTS!

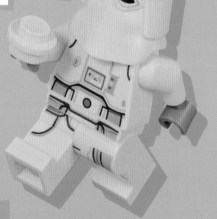

AT-AT ARMY

SNOWBALL-THROWING SNOWTROOPERS

USEFUL BRICKS

6X6 WEBBED INVERTED DISH

1X2 BRICK WITH AXLE HOLE

1X2 PLATE WITH TWO BARS

1X2 PLATE WITH SHOOTER

BUILDING IDEAS

ICY SNOWBALL LAUNCHER

CRATES TO HIDE BEHIND

HIDDEN TRIP WIRE

...THAT'S IT!

The Rebel Troopers decide to fight fire with snow. They build a snowball launcher and load it up. Ready, aim, splat! It's a bullseye. The AT-AT pilot loses control, and the vehicle wobbles and falls. Look out below!

WALKING TANKS

Could tanks on legs be used in real-life battles? It's unlikely. Their legs would be vulnerable to damage and the high center of gravity would make them unstable.

HAVE AN "ICE" DAY, PILOT!

Lever fires snowballs out of the launcher

Snowballs go in the 2x2 inverted dome

1

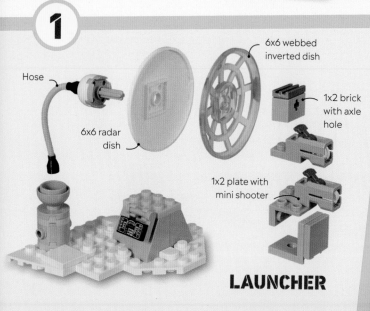

Hose

6x6 webbed inverted dish

6x6 radar dish

1x2 brick with axle hole

1x2 plate with mini shooter

LAUNCHER

2

ACTION SHOT

1x1 round plate

1x2 slope

1x2 plate with two bars

AT-AT HEAD

1x2 plate with clip

1x2 plate with handle

SNOWSTORM!
Crash! Down comes the AT-AT. Kori and her friend skedaddle just in time. Right into the path of a blizzard.

HOW TO BUILD!

Turbolasers

AT-AT has four legs made from cones

THAT SNOWBALL LAUNCHER IS "SNOW" JOKE.

2x4 tile covers entire side

HOW TO BUILD!

1x2 plate with rocks is jagged ice

BLINDING BLIZZARD

In the thick blizzard, Kori hears her comms unit ping. It's bad news. An Imperial fleet is nearing Hoth, and only a shield generator can stop it. Kori must get that part to base quickly, but it's miles away. What can she build?

THE PLAN = ?

OBSTACLES

HEAVY BLIZZARD

GRRRGLE!

FIERCE WAMPA

CHAIN

CROISSANT PIECE

1X2 PLATE WITH ROCKS

1X2/2X2 INVERTED BRACKET PLATE

VEHICLE EXHAUST PIPE

USEFUL BRICKS

BUILDING IDEAS

TAUNTAUN-DRAWN SLEIGH

STRONG SNOW PLOUGH

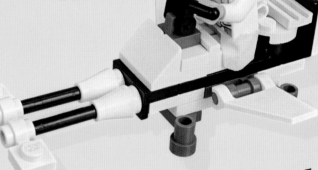

ZIPPY SNOW SPEEDER BIKE

...THAT'S IT!

A furry tauntaun wanders up, perfectly at home in the blizzard. Yuck! It smells awful, but it's eager to help. Kori and her friend build a sleigh and harness up the tauntaun. Hoth base here they come. Giddy-up!

WHAT'S THAT SMELL?

IT'S THE TAUNTAUN... HONEST!

Smooth sides let sleigh slide through the snow

Chain connects sleigh and tauntaun

URGENT! URGENT! WE NEED THAT MISSING PART NOW!

SLEIGH BELLS

On Earth, sleighs are pulled by horses. These snowy-weather vehicles can't stop quickly, so in the past, drivers put bells on the harness as a warning to others.

HOW TO BUILD!

1 SLEIGH

1x6 tile

1x2/2x2 inverted bracket plate

1x1 plate with clip

1x2 curved slope

Vehicle exhaust pipe with LEGO® Technic pin

2x2 curved slope

2

Croissant pieces are tauntaun horns

Pointy edges of plate are claws!

TAUNTAUN

1x2x3 slope brick

Croissant piece

1x1 tile

1x3 curved slope

1x1 brick with side stud

2x2x2 slope brick

1x2 plate with rocks

IN PIECES

Kori grabs the missing part, ready to hand over. Oren nudges her and points to the other pieces. Oops. The part has been crushed in the sleigh!

THE FINAL PIECE

The tauntaun team arrives at Hoth base. Kori explains that the missing part is damaged. Oh no! The part is the battery for the generator. Can Kori build something to fix the pesky piece to get the shield generator running before the Imperials arrive?

THE PLAN = ?

⚠ OBSTACLES

BROKEN GENERATOR BATTERY

INCOMING TROOPS

DON'T LET THEM TURN THAT SHIELD GENERATOR ON!

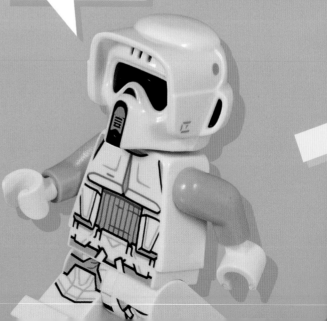

USEFUL BRICKS

BINOCULARS

1X2X²⁄₃ BRICK WITH STUDS ON THE SIDES

MECHANICAL ARM

1X1 SLOPE

TELESCOPE PIECE

1X1 ROUND TILE WITH BAR

1X1 ROUND PLATE

BUILDING IDEAS

TOOL-FILLED WORKSTATION

REPAIR DROID

...THAT'S IT!

Kori builds a repair droid, and it speeds into action. Ding! Bash! Whirr! The dented part is straightened, filed, polished. Then the battery is put back together and slotted into the shield generator. The generator is now activated!

INVISIBLE SHIELD

In *Star Wars*, a shield generator surrounds an area with an invisible force field that deflects attacks. Sadly, there are no real-life shield generators.

GO HOME, GUYS!

Broken battery piece from the shield generator

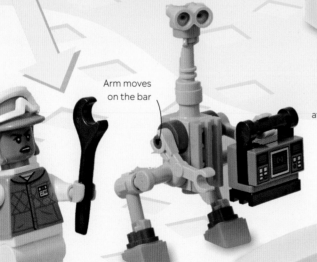

Arm moves on the bar

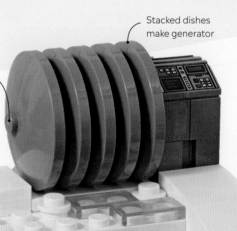

Stacked dishes make generator

Battery attaches to this stud

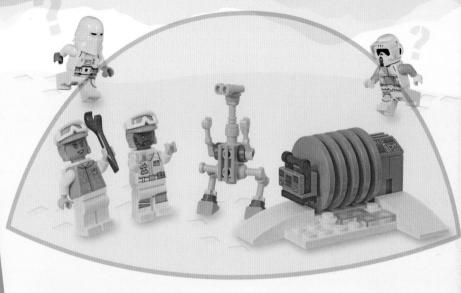

THEY'RE SHUTTING US OUT!

SAFE AT LAST
The shield encircles Hoth base with an invisible barrier that troopers just bounce off. Kori and her friends did it! They kept out the Imperials. Now it's time to celebrate.

HOW TO BUILD!

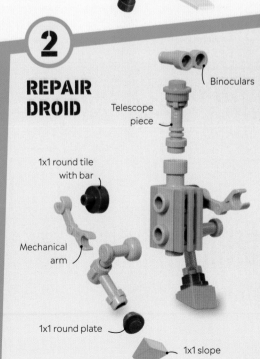

1

SHIELD GENERATOR

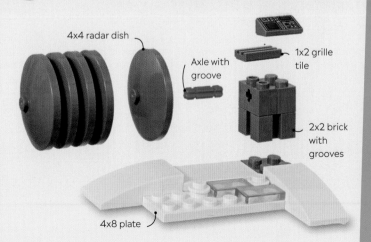

4x4 radar dish

Axle with groove

1x2 grille tile

2x2 brick with grooves

4x8 plate

2

REPAIR DROID

Binoculars

Telescope piece

1x1 round tile with bar

Mechanical arm

1x1 round plate

1x1 slope

MISSION COMPLETE

Turn up the music! Serve up the snacks! It's party time for the Rebels. Chewbacca has arrived. The tauntaun has stayed to celebrate. And there's R2-Z2C, with its new best friend, Yoda. The only ones missing from this party are the Imperials. Surely they didn't expect an invite?

ICE-CREAM CART

4x4 radar dish with pattern

Bar with stopper

1x1 plate with clip

2x2 tile

1x2 plate with bar

2x2x2 door with slot

2x2x2 box

HOW TO BUILD!

SHALL WE HIT THE DANCE FLOOR, OREN?

Lid on cart opens and closes

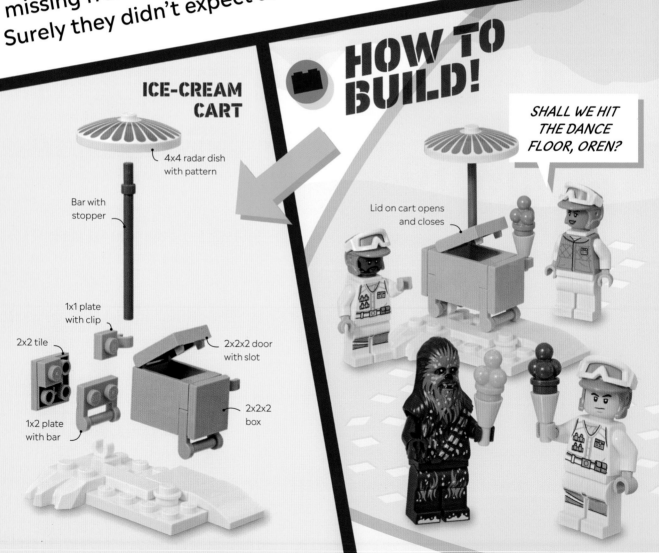

USEFUL BRICKS

BAR WITH STOPPER

1X1 PLATE WITH CLIP

2X2X2 BOX

2X2X2 DOOR WITH SLOT

1X2 PLATE WITH BAR

BUILDING IDEAS

SNACK TABLE

ICE-CREAM CART

DANCE FLOOR

1x1 tile tauntaun snout to eat ice cream!

SWAMP STEW IS THERE NOT?

1x1 half circle tile

Colorful transparent plates make the dance floor

WHAT AN ATMOSPHERE!

Pies and snacks fill the table

White wedge pieces are snowy ground

GLOSSARY

Aerobatics
Skillfully moving an aircraft, such as flying upside down or doing a loop-the-loop.

Crossfire
Shots being fired at an object from different directions.

Current
The movement of electricity, water, or air in one direction.

Deflect
A weight that acts as a balance to something else that has the same weight.

Dogfight
A fast and close fight between two aircraft.

Electromagnetic
Something which has both magnetic and electrical parts.

Extract
To take out or remove something.

Gravity
The natural force that pulls things toward each other. It is gravity that makes things fall to Earth.

Harness
A piece of equipment which is placed on an animal or object to control them or hold them in place.

Ignite
To begin a fire or cause something to explode.

Larva
A form of an insect that has left its egg but not yet developed into an adult.

Magnet
An object which can attract metal objects.

Predator
An animal that can hunt or eat other animals.

Prey
An animal that is hunted for food by another animal.

Program
To tell a device or system to operate in a particular way.

Propulsion
A force that pushes an object forward.

Resourceful
To be skilled at solving problems.

Ravenous
To be extremely hungry.

Trigeminal nerve
A group of long, thin structures like threads that carry information between the brain and parts of the face and jaw.

Unstable
To be likely to move or fall over.

Vapor
A gas or extremely small drops of liquid which are the result of heating a liquid or solid.

Vulnerable
If something is vulnerable it can be easily hurt or attacked.

MEET THE BUILDER
ROD GILLIES

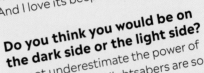

What is your favorite brick?

The 1x1 headlight brick—it's so useful and can be used to create some really interesting shapes.

Which LEGO® Star Wars™ character would you want to have as your sidekick?

It's got to be R2-D2. It would be such a useful pal to have around. And I love its beeps and whistles.

If you were a minifigure in this book, which build would you want to try out?

I love a puzzle, so I wouldn't mind trying to find my way around the droid distraction maze.

Do you think you would be on the dark side or the light side?

Do not underestimate the power of the dark side. Red lightsabers are so much cooler than green or blue ones!

Would you rather go skiing with the snowtroopers or tackle the obstacle course on Mustafar?

Absolutely the skiing. I'm not a fan of being too hot. Mustafar would be a step too far for me.

What would you like to eat and drink at the cantina on Tatooine?

Deep-fried Womp Rat with blue milk. It's a classic meal combo!

What LEGO® equipment would you want to have on a LEGO® Star Wars™ mission?

A big brick separator. Then I could disassemble anything in the world and put together whatever I needed.

Which LEGO® Star Wars™ ship would you want to drive in this mission?

I was really pleased with the mini model of the Star Destroyer. I'd love to take that for a spin!

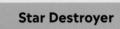

Star Destroyer

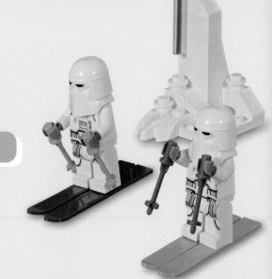

USEFUL BRICKS

All LEGO® bricks are useful, but some are more helpful than others when it comes to building on a galaxy mission! Don't worry if you don't have all of these parts. Be creative with the pieces you do have.

 Small parts and small balls can cause choking if swallowed. Not for children under 3 years.

BRICK BASICS

Bricks are the basis of most LEGO builds. They come in many shapes and sizes and are named according to size.

3

2x3 brick top view

2x3 brick side view

Plates are the same as bricks, only slimmer. Three stacked plates are the same height as a standard brick.

 1x2 plate

3 1x2 plates

1x2 brick

Tiles look like plates, but without any studs on top. This gives them a smooth look for more realistic builds.

 2x2 round tile

1x2 tile

Slopes are any bricks with diagonal angles. They can be big, small, curved, or inverted (upside-down).

1x2 inverted slope

1x3 curved slope

COOL CONNECTORS

Bricks don't have to be stacked. Connect elements in different ways using some of these pieces.

Any piece with a **bar** can fit onto a piece with a **clip**.

1x2 plate with handle

1x1 plate with clip

1x2 plate with bar

Jumper plates allow you to "jump" the usual grid of LEGO studs.

 1x2 jumper plate

 2x2 jumper plate

There are different kinds of **bricks with side studs**. They all allow you to build outward as well as upward.

 1x1 brick with one side stud

1x2x2 brick with four side studs

1x2/2x2 angle plate

THESE LOOK LIKE HANDY PIECES!

INTERESTING PIECES

Personalize your builds with some fun elements. Try adding food pieces, creatures, or anything that sparks your imagination.

Horn

Four-scoop ice-cream piece

Frog

Plant

Flame piece

Carrot and carrot top

Snowflake

Dinosaur tail

VEHICLE PARTS

Cars, trains, planes, and other things that go are helpful for getting out of trouble during an adventure. Here are some good parts for building vehicles.

2x2 plate with pins

3x3x2 cone

Console with steering wheel

Wheel with tire

1x2 plate with ball joint

1x2x3 transparent panel

Joystick

1x2 plate with socket

Propeller

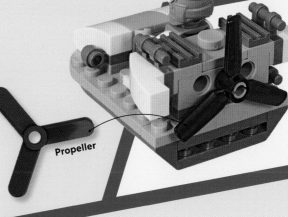

EQUIPMENT

Useful tools and gadgets come in handy for completing any mission. Make sure to build in plenty of things to help your minifigures on their way.

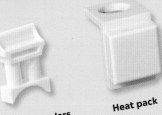

Electrobinoculars

Heat pack

HOW CAN WE USE THIS PIECE?

Wrench

Battery pack

Comms unit

DK | Penguin Random House

Senior Editor Tori Kosara
Senior Designer Lauren Adams
Editor Nicole Reynolds
Designer Isabelle Merry
Senior Production Editor Marc Staples
Senior Production Controller Lloyd Robertson
Managing Editor Paula Regan
Managing Art Editor Jo Connor
Publishing Director Mark Searle

Models designed and created by Rod Gillies
Additional models by Jason Briscoe, Nate Dias,
Jessica Farrell, Tim Goddard, Kevin Hall,
Rhys Knight, Barney Main, and Simon Pickard

Photography by Gary Ombler

Dorling Kindersley would like to thank: Ashley Blais, Randi Sørensen,
Heidi K. Jensen, Paul Hansford, Martin Leighton Lindhardt, and Nina Koopmann at the
LEGO Group; James McKeag for design assistance; Victoria Taylor for proofreading; and
Megan Douglass for Americanization.

First American Edition, 2023
Published in the United States by DK Publishing
1745 Broadway, 20th Floor, New York, NY 10019

Page design copyright ©2023 Dorling Kindersley Limited
DK, a Division of Penguin Random House LLC
23 24 25 26 27 10 9 8 7 6 5 4 3 2 1
001–326319–Sept/2023

Contains content previously published in LEGO® Epic History (2020), LEGO® Minifigure
Mission (2021), LEGO® Party Ideas (2022), LEGO® Star Wars™ Build Your Own Adventure
(2016), LEGO® Star Wars™ Build Your Own Adventure Galactic Missions (2019),
LEGO® Star Wars™ Ideas Book (2018), LEGO® Amazing Vehicles (2019)

A catalog record for this book is available from the Library of Congress.
ISBN 978-0-7440-8458-0
Library ISBN 978-0-7440-8459-7

Printed in China

For the curious
www.dk.com
www.LEGO.com/starwars
www.starwars.com

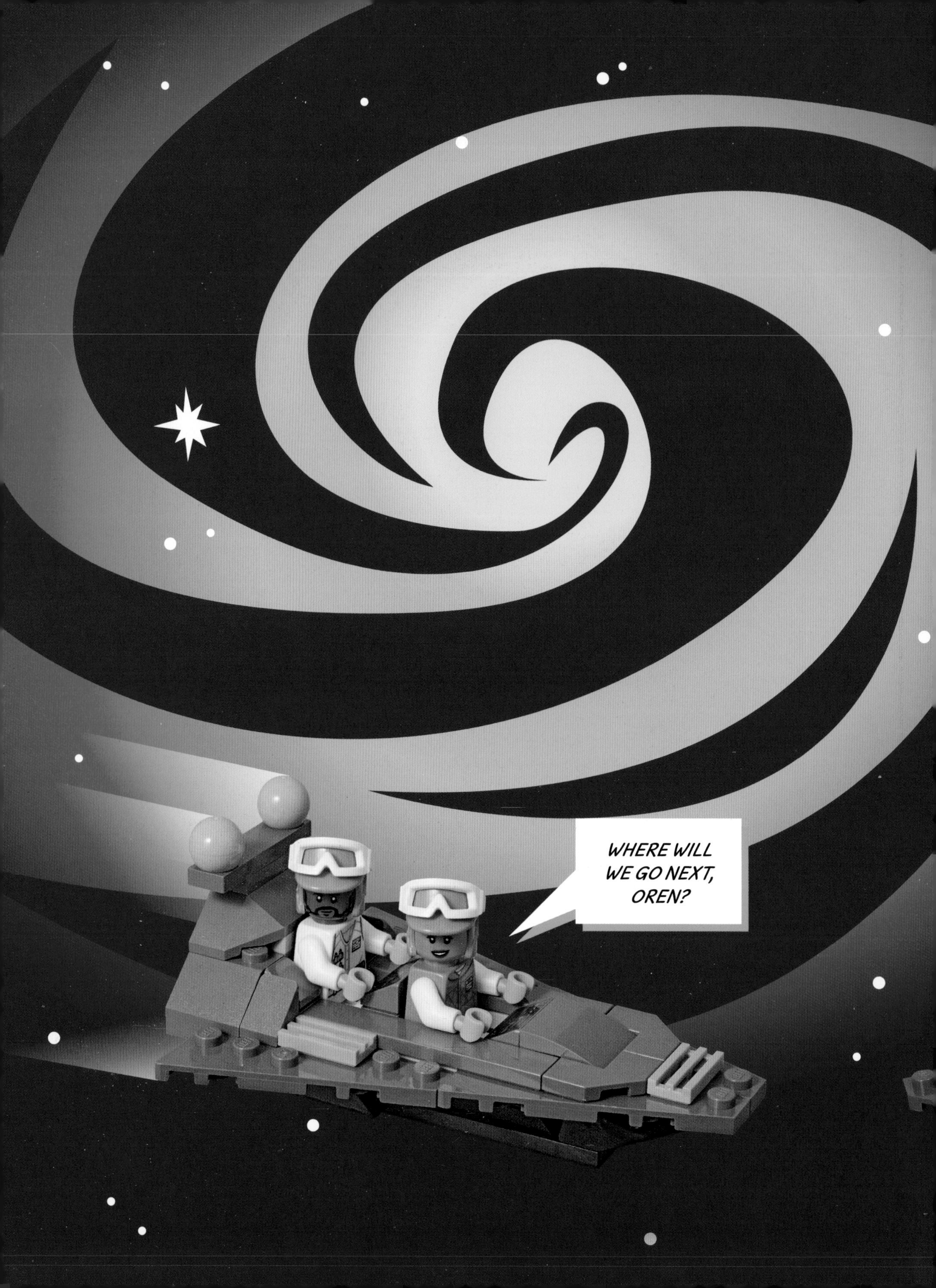
WHERE WILL WE GO NEXT, OREN?